Doggie Pants

Kelly Doudna

Illustrated by Anne Haberstroh

Consulting Editor, Diane Craig, M.A./Reading Specialist

ABDO
Publishing Company

Published by ABDO Publishing Company, 4940 Viking Drive, Edina, Minnesota 55435.

Printed in the United States.

Credits
Edited by: Pam Price
Curriculum Coordinator: Nancy Tuminelly
Cover and Interior Design and Production: Mighty Media
Photo Credits: AbleStock, Brand X Pictures, Corbis Images, ShutterStock, Thinkstock

Library of Congress Cataloging-in-Publication Data

Doudna, Kelly, 1963-
    Doggie pants / Kelly Doudna ; illustrated by Anne Haberstroh.
        p. cm. -- (Fact & fiction. Animal tales)
    Summary: During the dog days of summer, Sophie Dog hears about a yodeling contest for which the grand prize is a trip to a yodeling school in the Swiss Alps, and she convinces her best friend, Louise, to enter with her. Includes facts about dogs.
    ISBN 1-59679-931-5 (hardcover)
    ISBN 1-59679-932-3 (paperback)
    [1. Yodel and yodeling--Fiction. 2. Contests--Fiction. 3. Dogs--Fiction.] I. Haberstroh, Anne, ill.
II. Title. III. Series.

    PZ7.D74425Dog 2006
    [E]--dc22

                                                                                                    2005027830

SandCastle Level: Fluent

SandCastle™ books are created by a professional team of educators, reading specialists, and content developers around five essential components—phonemic awareness, phonics, vocabulary, text comprehension, and fluency—to assist young readers as they develop reading skills and strategies and increase their general knowledge. All books are written, reviewed, and leveled for guided reading, early reading intervention, and Accelerated Reader® programs for use in shared, guided, and independent reading and writing activities to support a balanced approach to literacy instruction. The SandCastle™ series has four levels that correspond to early literacy development. The levels help teachers and parents select appropriate books for young readers.

Emerging Readers
(no flags)

Beginning Readers
(1 flag)

Transitional Readers
(2 flags)

Fluent Readers
(3 flags)

These levels are meant only as a guide. All levels are subject to change.

FACT & FICTION

This series provides early fluent readers the opportunity to develop reading comprehension strategies and increase fluency. These books are appropriate for guided, shared, and independent reading.

FACT The left-hand pages incorporate realistic photographs to enhance readers' understanding of informational text.

FICTION The right-hand pages engage readers with an entertaining, narrative story that is supported by whimsical illustrations.

The Fact and Fiction pages can be read separately to improve comprehension through questioning, predicting, making inferences, and summarizing. They can also be read side-by-side, in spreads, which encourages students to explore and examine different writing styles.

FACT OR **FICTION?** This fun quiz helps reinforce students' understanding of what is real and not real.

SPEED READ The text-only version of each section includes word-count rulers for fluency practice and assessment.

GLOSSARY Higher-level vocabulary and concepts are defined in the glossary.

SandCastle™ would like to hear from you.

Tell us your stories about reading this book. What was your favorite page? Was there something hard that you needed help with? Share the ups and downs of learning to read. To get posted on the ABDO Publishing Company Web site, send us an e-mail at:

sandcastle@abdopublishing.com

Dogs pant to cool off. They inhale fresh, cool air and exhale warm air that carries away extra body heat.

It's the dog days of summer, and
Sophie Dog is on vacation from
school. It's too hot to fetch any sticks
or bury any bones. Instead, Sophie
just lies around panting and listening
to the radio.

Dogs can hear sounds up to four times farther away than humans can.

Sophie hears an ad on the radio for a yodeling contest. The grand prize is a trip to a yodeling school in the mountains of Switzerland. "I can yodel," Sophie thinks to herself. "Louise and I should enter that contest!"

7

Dogs howl, growl, grunt, whine, and bark
to communicate with each other.

Sophie phones her best friend, Louise, and tells her about the contest. "Bring your accordion over, and we will practice our act," Sophie says to Louise.

9

Many dogs howl along with sirens. Experts believe that dogs think sirens sound like other dogs howling.

As Sophie and Louise practice, the fire trucks leave from the station next door. The other dogs in the neighborhood howl, "Owooo, owooo, owoooooo!"

Sophie declares, "We sound so much better than that!"

11

Dogs can see a little color, but much less
vividly than humans do.

"We need something fun to wear," Sophie says. She and Louise go to a costume shop. "Look at these green lederhosen!" Sophie exclaims.

"They're perfect!" Louise agrees.

13

Dogs range in weight from under five pounds to over 200 pounds.

The day of the contest arrives.
Sophie sings, "Yodel-ay-hee-hoo."
Louise plays along on her accordion.
They sound better than all of the other
dogs. They easily win the grand prize.

15

Dogs see little detail but are very sensitive to movement.

Sophie and Louise look out the airplane windows at the mountains. They can barely contain their excitement as the airplane lands in Switzerland.

Dogs thrive on social play, whether it's with their human family or other dogs.

When Sophie and Louise arrive at the yodeling school, they join the crowd of dog yodelers who are already there.

"Oh Louise!" Sophie exclaims to her friend. "This is going to be so much fun!"

19

FACT OR FiCTiON?

Read each statement below. Then decide whether it's from the FACT section or the FiCTiON section!

1. Dogs can hear sounds up to four times farther away than humans can.

2. Dogs play the accordian.

3. Dogs can see a little color.

4. Dogs wear lederhosen.

Dogs pant to cool off. They inhale fresh, cool air   10
and exhale warm air that carries away extra body heat.   20

Dogs can hear sounds up to four times farther away   30
than humans can.   33

Dogs howl, growl, grunt, whine, and bark to   41
communicate with each other.   45

Many dogs howl along with sirens. Experts believe   53
that dogs think sirens sound like other dogs howling.   62

Dogs can see a little color, but much less vividly   72
than humans do.   75

Dogs range in weight from under five pounds to   84
over 200 pounds.   87

Dogs see little detail but are very sensitive to   96
movement.   97

Dogs thrive on social play, whether it's with their   106
human family or other dogs.   111

It's the dog days of summer, and Sophie Dog is on vacation from school. It's too hot to fetch any sticks or bury any bones. Instead, Sophie just lies around panting and listening to the radio.

Sophie hears an ad on the radio for a yodeling contest. The grand prize is a trip to a yodeling school in the mountains of Switzerland. "I can yodel," Sophie thinks to herself. "Louise and I should enter that contest!"

Sophie phones her best friend, Louise, and tells her about the contest. "Bring your accordion over, and we will practice our act," Sophie says to Louise.

As Sophie and Louise practice, the fire trucks leave from the station next door. The other dogs in the neighborhood howl, "Owooo, owooo, owoooooo!"

Sophie declares, "We sound so much better than that!"

"We need something fun to wear," Sophie says. 143
She and Louise go to a costume shop. "Look at 153
these green lederhosen!" Sophie exclaims. 158

"They're perfect!" Louise agrees. 162

The day of the contest arrives. Sophie sings, 170
"Yodel-ay-hee-hoo." Louise plays along on her 179
accordion. They sound better than all of the other 188
dogs. They easily win the grand prize. 195

Sophie and Louise look out the airplane windows 203
at the mountains. They can barely contain their 211
excitement as the airplane lands in Switzerland. 218

When Sophie and Louise arrive at the yodeling 226
school, they join the crowd of dog yodelers who are 236
already there. "Oh Louise!" Sophie exclaims to her 244
friend. "This is going to be so much fun!" 253

GLOSSARY

accordion. a handheld musical instrument that produces sound when air is forced through it by squeezing the two ends together

dog days. the period of hot weather between July and September

exhale. to breathe out

inhale. to breathe in

lederhosen. leather shorts with suspenders that are traditionally worn in the European Alps

yodel. to sing in a style that changes rapidly between normal tones and high, false tones

To see a complete list of SandCastle™ books and other nonfiction titles from ABDO Publishing Company, visit www.abdopublishing.com or contact us at: 4940 Viking Drive, Edina, Minnesota 55435 • 1-800-800-1312 • fax: 1-952-831-1632